FATHER & SUN

ROSS VICTORY

Created by J. Ross Victory
rossvictory.com

Cover illustration by David Izaguirre, Jr.
izythereal.com

Cover graphic design and color by William Sikora III
sikoraentertainment.com

Edited by Kaylee Robinson and Joshua Powell

Proofread by Kate Seger

Special thanks to all the beta readers
ISBN 13: 978-1-63752-301-8 (paperback)
ISBN 13: 978-1-63752-302-5 (e-book)
https://www.rossvictory.com
viewsfromthecockpitbook@gmail.com

FATHER & SUN DESCRIPTION

Trey Amana, a forty-something, hardworking father of two, discovered his dad's death five years ago on the day after Christmas. Although Trey has grieved and prioritized his health, holiday music and decorations trigger painful memories. To take the final step toward healing the loss while saving extra cash for his holiday-obsessed kids, Trey decides to close his late father's storage unit once and for all.

Trey discovers a journal written during his father's college years. His dad, Art, reveals an outrageous family secret driving Trey into a wormhole of suspicions. With family members en-route to Trey's home, Trey is burdened by the need for answers while somehow producing a hospitable Christmas.

Father & Sun explores how secrets and well-meaning motivations from the past can have a counteractive generational impact.

Father & Sun contemplates life in the shadows or life standing on the Sun (owning one's truth), speaking to the passing of the torch from father to son, what it means to be honorable, and the spiritual, emotional, and mental effect on heirs.

TRIGGER WARNINGS: Adult Language

"To love and be loved is to feel the sun from both sides."

David Viscott

CONTENTS

ALL I WANT FOR CHRISTMAS IS

What would you do with a million-dollar budget for Christmas decorations? A life-sized snow globe? A Christmas colored pyrotechnics show? How about live-in carolers that sing and shut up on demand?

While I don't have an enormous budget, middle-of-the-road has never described Christmas decorations in my home. Growing up, I spent Christmas Eve and Christmas Day in a church pew listening to a sweaty, overcaffeinated pastor guilt the congregation about giving their money to him instead of the local department store. I vowed that every Christmas would be over the top, and this year there was no exception.

Thirty packs of flickering, white holiday lights surround the house. Battery-operated candles in every window. Tinsel, garland, bows, and ribbons in the front yard's bushes and trees. A six-foot inflatable snowman along with *black* Santa—fueling my passive rebellion—his reindeer on the roof, and we still had space for the nativity scene, The Grinch, *and* Spongebob.

My son, Avery, and I created a festive scene without breaking any body parts. After completing the Fall semester with a 4.0 GPA and a winning lacrosse season, my wife, Saben, and I granted our son's wish for an over-the-top Christmas.

Saben, Caleb, my youngest son nicknamed *Biscuit*—because he was obsessed with Pillsbury Southern Homestyle Biscuits—transformed the inside of our home into a photoshoot-ready winter wonderland.

Our living room boasted an eight-foot, flocked Balsam-fir tree and a 100-foot long vintage train set that circled the edge of the ceiling, with holiday music, pinecones, and string lights in every direction. With Christmas a week away, I could not escape one thing—the fifth anniversary of my father's death. Arthur "Art" Amana died on the twenty-sixth of December five years ago.

The sight of his body becoming a deflated flesh bag, was etched in my mind. He had transformed into an unpicked grape on a vine. I often wondered what I had done to deserve such horrifying memories. After years of separating myself from his church, I prayed again when he died—one last time. I waited for a reason. I needed to know why he died alone with no family around. I heard nothing like usual.

My father was a vibrant, stubborn man. He was opinionated and had a zest for life. He was someone who could sell water to a well; he was just that personable and persuasive. He often had the loudest, most unpopular opinion in our neighborhood barbershop, and somehow, everyone agreed with him by the time they left.

Sometimes I don't know if my grief, which sometimes feels like anger, stemmed from watching cancer suck the life out of him or if it was actual rage. Rage at the reality that Dad didn't tell anyone about his fatal diagnosis. As his son, I felt like I was entitled to that information. One day he was here; the next, he was gone.

Grief has schizophrenic qualities. Some days, I woke up awkwardly feeling relieved that the old man was dead. Relieved that I didn't have to listen to him rant about how the world was going to hell. I didn't have to listen to him handpick scriptures about whatever *he* was going through that day. I didn't have to pretend like listening to a seventy-something-year-old's desire to grope a twenty-year-old college girl in his apartment building was normal. Some days, I felt free—like a burden had been lifted.

Most days, most of those five years, I felt a gap in my heart—like I was being vacuumed into a black hole. Like I had been dropping on a roller coaster for a thousand years. My kids would likely not remember attending their grandfather's funeral, and they would never know the man himself. I felt a hole of fear—the fear of having to be a father with no council.

Dad and my mom, Susan, had nearly forty-five years of marriage before they divorced. My sister, Tiana, and I still speculate about what happened. It happened fast, via e-mail, with no explanation. As a forty-year-old man with my own family, I was not necessarily interested in the details, but no information was offered up, even from my father. Although we weren't the best friends ever, I thought it would be realistic to assume he'd share the reason with his adult, married son. Tiana and I would speculate for hours, making up stories to make us feel better.

Having been married ten years, I thought that there would have been a solid decade after forty years of marriage, maybe a decade and half of faking it. My wife Saben is beautiful. She's funny, intelligent, emotionally sharp, keeps her body neat, and is an enthusiastic lover plus some.

But most married people know, love is one piece of a pie. Sex is another piece. Business, financial, personal, political gains are other real pieces of marriage and family. And if my parents could not crack the code after forty years, what did that mean for my obsession with making this whole *black family thing* work? And *who* was I trying to make it work for?

My Uncle Charles, Dad's only older brother, had introduced my parents in college. Before my parents graduated with their Bachelors, they got married and became pregnant with me. Two years later, Tiana arrived. My mom was the only child, so Uncle Charles and my grandparents were our only extended family.

Although we did not go to private schools, my dad and my mom funded our college careers by saving most of their income. Unlike other kids in our neighborhood, Tiana and I enjoyed brand-new toys that operated adequately. And my parents never had their possessions repossessed like our neighbors.

I don't recall either of my parents taking days off work. We Amanas weren't wealthy enough to take an overseas vacation. Uncle Charles was reasonably well off, and if the rumors were true, he had made over a million dollars gambling. Growing up, he lent us his cabin in the mountains. Escaping to the hills for the 4th of July and Memorial Day felt like Tiana and I had gone somewhere far away as little kids.

When I became a father with Avery, I instinctively understood that my parents were not perfect. I obsessed about how Avery would view me as a father. Would he think I was the Hulk or an earthworm? Would I be the first person he called or the person he forgot to call? I found the expectation of fatherly perfection debilitating due to navigating the relationship with my dad.

Growing up, I was often the last child to be picked up from after school care. My dad was supposed to pick me up from school, and a handful of times, he forgot. Every time he failed, a creepy teacher's aide called Bernie dropped me off at home. There was a rumor around school that Bernie had gone to jail.

I remember Bernie joked that he could drive off with me, and no one would ever know. I can still feel fear and sense of helplessness from Bernie's comments. Being forgotten at school was embarrassing and terrifying, and all my dad said was that 'he forgot.'

But now, I understand how adults get caught up. I get caught up in work and stuck in my head. Sometimes I forget to tell Saben my plans, and sometimes I'm just exhausted. What if I forget to pick up Avery, and he gets traumatized mentally or physically and never tells me? What if he perceives my earnest attempt to do something and be there as an assassination on his life?

I vowed to give my kids the best education, protect their emotions, and prioritize a global mindset. The pressure of being a Black man with a Black family in America was enormous.

Pressure from messages promoted in media about my life's value, pressure to balance emotional strength with vulnerability, pressure to stay employed so we don't become homeless—I always felt like there was a choir of invisible people waiting to rejoice if I messed up. Most days, I could not decipher if this pressure was self-inflicted or actually occurring.

With a small family, everything I was building felt like it was put under the microscope by my parents. There was a silent expectation to do what they do how they do it. Perhaps I overthought passive-aggressive comments or interpreted silence as rejection or opposition, but it felt real.

"Hun...you ok?" my wife, Saben, asked, rubbing my back as I stared into our large bathroom vanity, brushing my teeth.

"Why did we agree to have Christmas here again?" I asked.

"Good question..." Saben took off her robe and got into the shower.

"Is it too late to cancel?" I asked jokingly.

"Oh my god, Trey! We have almost twenty people coming. We can't cancel."

"My eggnog is gonna be spiked the whole time," I jested.

"Trey!"

"Unc Charles with his loud ass mouth. He's just like dad, but the ignorant rich version. My mom and her conspiracies. All at once, it's too much."

"Well, your mom is bringing her friend. And your sister will be here too. Is Tiana still with... what's her name?" Saben asked.

"Debbie? Yes. But I don't know, Sabe. Unc Charles, my mom, Debbie...shoot me now."

"I'm sure your mom will bring that banana pudding, though. Since my parents can't fly in, it's gonna be potluck style. We can cook next year."

I could hear Avery and Biscuit yelling in the living room as I complained to Saben about the Christmas guest list and our $600 electric bill.

"I'm still getting charged $100 a month for dad's storage. It's about time I go through all that stuff. We can save a hundred there."

After five years, I still hadn't gone through my dad's storage unit. His death happened unusually quick, and I was so busy being a lawyer, a husband, and a father that his storage sat untouched.

He lived two hundred miles away from us in the small city of Fisherman's Lake. He rented a modest one-bedroom apartment in a two-story, twenty-unit apartment building. He was found dead by his neighbor. He had invited me to visit for years, and I never made it. Looking back, the closer his death became, the more frequent the requests were. But I never went.

"Dad!" Avery yelled.

"What?"

"Caleb knocked down the tree."

"No, I didn't," Biscuit responded.

"Biscuit, are you breaking stuff?" I could hear the boys arguing.

At ten years old, Avery was my helper. Everywhere I went, he wanted to go. Any and all questions came to me. He didn't ask normal kid questions like *Is Santa Claus real* or *Where do babies come from.* Avery asked questions like *Why do people use money instead of something else* and *What is God.*

Avery was highly confident and a strategic thinker, yet he rarely made decisions for himself with me around. In order to promote independence, I sought to guide him and simultaneously encourage him to trust his own judgment and experience.

I enjoyed spending time with Avery and talking in depth about his interpretations of the world, which was more than my dad had ever done for me. Avery had taken an interest in astronomy. He was curious about the rings of Saturn, obsessed with the moons of Jupiter. At least once a week, we would set up a camp in our backyard on a clear night, with blankets, popcorn, and juice boxes, and stargaze, imaging celestial objects light-years away. One night, Avery asked me *Where did grandpa go when he died.* The best answer I had was that grandpa became a star. He became a sun for planets far, far away, which Avery accepted.

Avery's idolization of me scared me. Something about his eyes made me feel inadequate and acutely aware of my imperfections. If Avery put me on a pedestal, I would surely fall or be deemed ignorant to some key detail in his experience. Instead of pushing him away, I tried to live with the emotional discomfort and bring him in closer.

Seven-year-old Biscuit was a mama's boy with an empathetic heart. He was an artist. He loved fast and crashed hard. Biscuit had a rare sensitivity that Saben and I wanted to preserve.

I was determined to teach him how to fight since I could not guarantee that he would not become a target for being a compassionate boy. I told Biscuit that if someone called him out of his name or touched him inappropriately, he should give them one strong verbal warning and a hard shove.

I instructed Biscuit, if they disrespect him again, strike them in the face, or tell them that his dad fights children of any age, and I will beat their ass.

Saben felt that teaching Biscuit how to fight, and be brash, was a negative approach to defend his soft nature. Saben was homeschooled most of her life and never spent time on a schoolyard. Teaching my sons how to fight was a smart response in a cruel, unforgiving society.

In my first year of high school, my parents moved, forcing us to change schools. My old school was mostly Black kids, but my new school was incredibly racially diverse. The first few months, Tiana and I tried to mix in with the Black kids, thinking we'd be most welcomed by people who looked like us.

Our whole high school career, the Black kids made comments about how we spoke white or thought we were white people. Tiana liked to read books and ride horses. I was on the debate team and ran cross country. We were nerdy, but our Black parents never made us feel anything other than Black. My parents were devoted to our education and keeping us out of jail. We did not understand why they felt betrayed by our presence. Eventually, Tiana and I made friends with kids who enjoyed the things we liked.

There was an incident where a kid named Maal called out to us, "here come Aunty and Uncle Tom," and began making kissy sounds. Maal then called Tiana "a high yellow house nigger," at which the other Black kids exploded in laughter.

Fed up, I threw my elbow into Maal's face breaking his nose. Maal and I were suspended for one week. Gossip spread that two Black boys had been fighting—and I was one of them—creating awkwardness between me, other students, and my teachers.

My parents assumed that the kids were jealous of us, and it was my temper that needed to be corrected. I could not imagine Biscuit being bullied for being himself. I could not conceive a child with a heart as big as my son's, allowing others to tell him who he is and who he is not. I would never allow Biscuit, or Avery, to experience feeling othered. Especially from people who claim to have their back.

I continued speaking to Saben, "I'll drive out to Fisherman's Saturday and go through it. Maybe drop some stuff at Goodwill and close it up."

"It's been five years next week. Do you want to talk about it?" Saben asked from inside the shower.

"Five years," I reflected, "I still don't get why he wouldn't tell anyone."

"Trey, you know your dad was a prideful man. He was probably embarrassed. Maybe scared of what you would think," Saben paused.

We discussed what it must have felt like to receive a fatal diagnosis and keep it secret for several minutes.

The hypnotic trickle of the shower water distracted me momentarily. Saben continued, "What men, *Black* men, do you know who discuss their feelings, not to mention their health needs, besides you?"

Saben always had a way of reminding me of something I had not considered or had forgotten. I remembered that accepting the loss of my father had opened the door to making changes to my life, starting with the state of my emotional life.

Who am I as a man compared to him? Who am I as a father compared to him? What does my generation know now that he didn't? I had to define these things for myself, and I was deeply committed to not repeating the pain he had caused by not investing emotionally or hiding things that might affect my family.

"I'm so glad I married you," I laughed. "Closing up the storage is the last thing I gotta do. I can feel it."

Saben thrust her butt against the fogging shower glass. She turned around and pressed her pussy against the glass, eyeballing me intensely.

"Ok, you're playin'," I locked the bathroom door. "Need some company in there?"

FISHERMAN'S LAKE

With Christmas seven days away and my dad's death anniversary on December twenty-sixth, I decided to drive out to Fisherman's Lake. To reflect, to reminisce, and to close up his storage unit once and for all. Nothing could prepare me for what I would find.

Fisherman's Lake was a sleepy town two hundred miles outside of the city. Fisherman's Lake was famous for Rainbow trout and duck frites, and the long line of homely family-owned restaurants offering tourists trout in one of two options – pan-fried or baked garlic butter. Known for its trout, it was also a thriving weekend spot for college kids to kayak and hold parties on boats. My dad had moved to Fisherman's Lake a year after he and my mom divorced.

I reflected on memories from my childhood as I drove. My dad had attended all of my junior league football games. He was a recognizable face at Parent-Teacher conferences. He had even picked me up from the police station when I had been arrested for petty theft after the Maal incident and agreed not to tell my mom as long as I paid the $500 fine.

Despite these memories, I could not glean if my dad actually approved of me—if he liked me as a man—as Trey Amana, not as his son. He never told me he loved me. I never heard him say he loved anyone or anything.

He never asked how I got along with Saben, though he occasionally asked how my kids were doing. Still, he never dug deep about my thoughts surrounding their birth on a fatherly level—my thoughts about becoming responsible for two living beings and my ability to provide for them. I only noticed all of this after he died.

Even when I volunteered details from my life, he was not concerned, and it felt like a waste of time. I did what I thought he would approve of. Even after his death, the impulse to pick up the phone to call him remained for years.

The Sun began to set behind the Rocky Mountains as I arrived at Fisherman's Lake. I had never seen a sunset so marvelous—like someone had taken leftover pastel watercolors and threw them into the sky to land on whichever cloud they chose. The storage unit had closed when I arrived.

There were only two hotels in Fisherman's Lake, both fully occupied, leaving the only option of a sleazy *by-the-hour* motel across the street from the storage unit. The motel's office was a drive-thru window covered in black, one-way glass.

The beds were king-sized and heart-shaped with large crusty mirrors on the ceiling, and nearly every TV channel was 1980's style porn. I purchased twenty-four hours and had the misfortune of forgetting to bring my own bed sheets. I made it two hours before deciding to sleep in my car.

The next day

"Good morning. Can I help you?"

A smiley customer service agent greeted me as I walked into the storage lobby, cracking and massaging my neck.

"Stayed across the street?" the agent asked.

"You can tell?"

"Most people don't stay there for longer than two hours."

I presented her with my dad's death certificate and explained that I wanted to close down the unit before Christmas. The agent confirmed that my name and Tiana's name had been listed as emergency contacts. The clerk gave me instructions and keys to access the unit, sharing that she had seen my dad a few times and described him as a sweet old man.

"Wow," I mumbled to myself, looking around his space.

My dad had rented a ten-foot-by-ten-foot unit. It was very organized, filled with old clothes, photo albums in boxes categorized by decade, books in boxes, and furniture from our childhood home.

I inspected the items, separating keepsakes from donations. My dad had collected suits over the years, all in decent condition that could be donated. I smiled, reminiscing there was never a time he was not wearing a suit.

Two hours turned to four hours. Four hours turned to six. I took a lunch break to taste-test the pan-fried trout and duck frites everyone raved about. It was just as disgusting as the motel room.

Throughout the day, I texted photos of our childhood to my sister.

"OMG! Our family was so cute," Tiana responded.

"So much history in here. A lot of life. But, isn't it normal to tell someone you're sick?" I asked.

"We'll never know that, Trey. The fact is, he didn't tell us for a reason."

"He's obligated to tell his KIDS!"

"Is he?" Tiana asked. *"Is anyone obligated to do anything?"*

"For your family, YES!" I responded.

"What if you don't like your family? What if your family are criminals? What if your family can't be trusted?" Tiana asked.

"Well, you don't have kids, so you don't know."

"Noone is obligated to do anything, not cha mama, not cha daddy, not you, not me..." Tiana wrote.

"Guess we're different."

"Yeah, I guess, so," I responded.

We texted for several hours, remembering moments with our grandparents and those timeless memories in Uncle Charles' cabin.

"Ugh! I miss Dad so much."

"Me, too," I responded.

"How's it goin'?" Saben texted.

"Pretty good. Probably need another day to drop off clothes and furniture. I have one more box to go through."

By the end of my first night in Fisherman's Lake, I had condensed most of the photos into three large boxes. The last box was labeled for college years. It was filled with pictures of random people I had never known, science fairs, and photos of college parties.

I texted Tiana, *"Look at Dad gettin' lit."*

"OMG!" she responded.

There were photos of him and Unc Charles receiving their Bachelor's degrees, with all four of my grandparents smiling from ear to ear. I had forgotten that my parents were capable of youthful energy and there once existed a time when they did not know each other.

Buried between the photo albums was a spiral-bound journal—the first journal I had seen in my dad's belongings. I debated if I should open it. I had never written a journal, but I imagined that people write journals not to be found.

I examined the journal for a few seconds before opening it to read the first page. I learned that my dad was not a fan of college and hated accounting. He had gotten a chance to meet and greet Malcolm X at his college in the early 60s, which he described as magical and affirming.

Then, I got to page twelve. Life-changing page twelve. On page twelve, reading the first sentence felt like I had awakened and seen a family of elves flying through my house sprinkling fairy dust, or our family portraits had begun chatting with each other through the walls. The words were eerie, confusing; unfathomable.

Today, my girlfriend of one year, Susan, confessed that she slept with my brother and is pregnant.

I reread the sentence.

Today, my girlfriend of one year, Susan, confessed that she slept with my brother and is pregnant.

I read it again and again.

Susan sobbed uncontrollably, confessing her love for me. She said she was drunk, and Charlie pushed himself on her. He knows what Susan means to me. He has his pick of women. But I'm confused because Susan told me that she didn't want to have sex until we were married. It would have been our first time.

I continued reading.

Susan is terrified of her pastor father. She's caught him hitting her mom. He's a bit fiery and would surely beat her badly. She asked me to marry her before she began showing. She promised to be the best wife.

"What the hell?" I repeated under my breath.

I confronted my brother. I struck him hard. The devil was in me. He didn't hit me back. When I calmed down, Charlie

24

said not to marry her because she offered herself to him; she was easy and a digger. He said he could tell it wasn't her first time because he's been with seven women. Please, God, help me.

Strange sensations developed in my body. I felt a mix of nausea and mental hysteria, almost like my head was going to pop off. I wanted to holler and kick, but at the same time, I was too confused and paralyzed to move. I shut the journal. I couldn't shoulder any more words from my father.

Then, I opened it.

I closed it again. Should I tell Tiana? Should I tell Saben?

I opened the journal and took a photo of page twelve, and texted it to Tiana. She called me almost immediately on video chat with her mouth covered.

"Trey, what the f*ck?"

"Trey!" she wrote. "You need to call Mom NOW. What the f*ck is he talking about?"

"I can't call her."

"Well, I will," Tiana said.

"No, please don't. Just," I had no words.

Tiana sat in silence with me, contemplating the probability that the journal was not accurate. But the dates matched perfectly. Almost nine months later, to the day, I was born. Nearly a month later, my parents were married.

"She could easily wear a cute wedding dress, without anyone knowing she's pregnant. Actually, I have a photo of the wedding right here. LOOK! That's me in there." I put a wedding photo of our parents in the camera.

"OH. MY. GOD. And that lady swears her shit don't stink," Tiana responded. "It makes sense, right? Unc Charles and Dad never talked. Did you ever see them talking like brothers? He wasn't at their wedding either."

Tiana went down the wormhole of possibilities.

"Tiana, speculating is making me feel worse."

"But it makes sense, right? Mom was probably f*ckin' Uncle Charles our whole life. What if they had some kind of secret thrupple agreement? Actually, what if they divorced because dad had enough? OMG, what if Uncle Charles is my daddy, too?" Tiana said.

I hung up the phone on Tiana. I sent her to voicemail each time she called back. I texted Saben to let her know that a discovery had been made, and we must discuss it when I get back. I packed up the remaining items and slept in my car again.

The next morning, unable to comprehend what happened, and with another crook in my neck, I drove by my dad's apartment building to see where he lived. My head raced with ideas as I drove. *I wondered if my dad pretended to like me to keep the family together? Did he resent me? Was the disconnect I felt because I was not his biological son?*

I pulled up to my dad's apartment building. The building was freshly painted dark green with a small five-foot manicured lawn. A seventy-something-year-old man sat outside the front door on a bench, smoking a large Half Bent Billiard pipe. The man mad-dogged me as I approached the building. I scanned the intercom list of residents.

"Manager is 101," the man said, irritated.

"Not here for the manager. My dad used to live here. Arthur Amana."

The man took another puff of his pipe, squinting his eyes looking me up and down.

"Are you Trey? Trey Amana?"

"Yes."

The man's attitude relaxed. "Ya daddy was my neighbor. I'm Robert J. Collin, Sr. I found ya daddy."

I shook Mr. Collin's hand and thanked him for calling the paramedics. He invited me to sit down and offered me a handful of his green grapes. Mr. Collin explained that he had tried to resuscitate my dad.

"Some days, I wake up and still think ya daddy lives here. He was good at fishin' and can pan-fry the hell out of some trout."

Mr. Collin recounted memories he had with my father, which felt like a good friendship. Both men, retired, living alone, had spent hours and hours talking and fishing and had gotten to know each other very well.

"And boy, oh boy, he loved you and ya sister. That's all he talked about. My kids down in North Carolina, six grandbabies, don't even remember my birthday. I loved hearin' how ya'll grew up."

Mr. Collin informed me that he knew everything. Everything. Still, he was polite enough not to describe what he knew, often scanning my face as we spoke before making his next comment. I told him that I had returned to the area to pack up my dad's storage unit.

I showed him photos of Saben, Avery, and Biscuit. He engaged the photos with playfulness. Mr. Collin informed me that my dad discovered he had Stage 4 cancer six months before he passed. My dad had told him and my mom he was given one year but made it six months.

"My mom knew?" I asked.

"Son, yo mama is a cold piece. He told her first and me second. Made us promise not to tell, swear on our kids."

I texted Tiana as he spoke. "Mom knew dad was sick." Followed by, "I'm done with this family."

The sun began to set as Mr. Collin and I completed our conversation. The sky filled up with water-colored clouds. I offered him my dad's old suits.

"Boy, do I look like I have anywhere to go? It's me, this pipe, and this Lake until it's over." Mr. Collin took a long draw of tobacco.

I got up to leave. As I walked away, Mr. Collin called out, "Son, your daddy loved you. More than a child can understand, more than he could say to you, and I know what that feels like. Maybe you understand with those kiddies you got." My lips curled in to smile, waving goodbye to Mr. Collin politely.

During the drive home, I put Saben on video chat and explained everything that had occurred. I pulled over multiple times in fits of anger, sadness, and disbelief that my world was folding in on itself.

"I think I have to go to the psychiatric ward or somethin'," I told Saben. "I don't feel ok."

Saben offered to pick me up as I hollered on the side of the road, which I refused. Without her warnings to pull my car over on the highway, I would have crashed. A three-hour drive turned into a six and half hour drive.

"I'm so glad you married me, Sabe."

With twenty Christmas guests beginning their migration to our home, I asked Saben to injure me. I wanted her to put me into the ER with a severe injury to prevent visitors. Mr. Collin had made me believe that my dad loved me despite all that occurred, but I was tormented by what would happen next. *What happens when you find out the man you called dad for forty years isn't your dad, and he's dead? What happens when Christmas is two days away?* After visiting Fisherman's Lake, I convinced myself that the Amanas were cursed.

MERRY CHRISTMAS

Christmas morning arrived. Within two days, Saben and I had purchased, hidden, and wrapped all of our kids' gifts, including hiding a four-month-old chocolate Labrador in our closet. The puppy peed in every section of the closet and managed to aim pebble-sized turds into the thousand-dollar Tanino Crisci loafers Saben had purchased me for my fortieth birthday.

The morning started with Avery and Biscuit running down the stairs screaming in excitement to see the puppy wearing a bright red leash and discovering that they had received everything on their list. Avery shrieked out in excitement when he opened his Celestron telescope and binocular set.

Biscuit rejoiced to discover his Kiddie Jam music studio. Preparing for Christmas had helped me compartmentalize the parallel universe I found myself in. Saben and I left the kids opening gifts and managed to get in a passionate quickie before our long, arduous day.

I made it a tradition to start Christmas day by making salmon croquettes with fresh fruit, green smoothies, and English tea cakes with my kids. Everyone wore their ugly sweater and brought a list of five things they were thankful for in the year.

Throughout the morning, cousins and extended family arrived. Every guest was stunned by the decorations in my home, taking photos all over the house and posting them on social media.

It had been several months since I had seen my mother and years since I had seen Unc Charles. Saben had been in touch with both of them for the plans for the day. Unc Charles had arrived quietly, disappearing to play with Avery, Biscuit, and the new puppy.

Our doorbell rang ten minutes after noon for the last grand entrance.

"Can you get it?" I looked over at Saben in deep contemplation as Avery and Biscuit helped me flour the teacake dough and fill the scoops with dried fruit.

My mom, her friend Cletus, and my mom's mom, grandma Bernadine (Gammy), who was approaching one hundred years old, made an extravagant entrance. My mom boisterously commented on the decorations, comparing each one to better-branded decorations in her home. I could hear her approaching the kitchen. I greeted her and managed to avoid being in the same room for an hour. She finally appeared behind me in the kitchen.

"Dear, why is Saben using dishes for the food? With all these people I would use paper. Kids don't need dishes."

My mom began to critique my home and my family, giving backhanded compliments to guests that walked by for the bathroom.

"Are there gang members here?" my mom asked, clutching her over-sized Louis Vuitton purse.

"I don't know, Mom. Probably. I don't know."

My mother began to talk about Avery, "Every time I see Avery, he looks like a swamp creature, like he's been fighting bears in the forest."

"And Trey," she reached for her phone, "Is this *nail* polish on Biscuit's nails?" My mom leaned in, rubbing my shoulder, showing me a photo she had taken of Biscuit's nails. "Is this the direction we're going?"

My muscles began to twitch. The love affair with Uncle Charles, or at least a fling by my dad's estimate, mixed with her commentary nearly put me over the edge. High-pitched voices in my head repeated, "page twelve, page twelve, page twelve." I breathed in through my nose and out through my mouth, trying to recall Saben's calming techniques.

I changed the topic and pulled away, "Sabe and Biscuit did great with the tree this year, didn't they?"

I paced over to the oven to check on the turkey.

"Trey, do we know if your sister's bringing a boy or a girl this year?" My mom giggled, scrolling through photos on her phone. "That girl," she raised her eyebrows and threw her neck back in suspicion. "What she call herself last year?"

"Tiana is *bisexual,* and she's bringing her girlfriend Debbie," I responded.

A few feet away in the hallway, Uncle Charles' ears perked up.

"Girlfriend," my mom motioned in air quotes. "If she's bisexual, wouldn't it be easier for her to...focus on the male half – why oppress yourself?"

"Easier for who?" I asked.

"All of that brings unnecessary attention," my mom said, applying foundation to her face.

"Sho 'nuff," Uncle Charles interjected. "I think they puttin' something in the water. All that EBGT stuff is unnatural."

"A pastor at my church said someplace found a cure. His son has that, too," my mom continued. "Maybe him and Tiana should meet. Two bisexuals make them straight, right? Is that how that works?" my mom giggled putting her hands together like a sandwich.

"Tiana is with Debbie," I repeated.

"Jesus said Adam and Eve, not Adam, Eve, Steve, Debra, Joe, but he really Kim...am I lyin'? Make it make sense," Unc Charles said.

I motioned Saben into the living room, leaving my mom and Unc Charles talking.

"Sabe, I can't do it." I cracked every knuckle in my hands, Saben concentrating in deep concern. I began to pant and breathe rapidly. Sabe pulled me in.

"Your kids need you to. Your dad needs you to. I need you to."

"Forty years?" I chuckled. "And my dad? I hope you mean Art and not that clown in there. You see that look on his face? You can't tell if he's always surprised or always constipated."

Saben offered calming words. Soon after, the doorbell rang.

"Aunty Tiana!" Avery and Biscuit exploded with happiness, rushing to the door to hug my sister, who was with her girlfriend, Debbie. "Aunty Debbie!" they cheered.

Tiana and I gave each other the eye and fist-bumped. I hugged Debbie, who was with her nephew Fernando.

"This house is something serious, Trey. I'm sure y'all won whatever contest, haha." Tiana began to scan the decorations. "Our parents would never..."

I scoffed, "Exactly the point. I'm doing everything opposite of "the Amana's," I mocked.

Debbie and Fernando began to walk toward the kitchen.

"Hey y"all, don't go in the kitchen." Tiana looked puzzled. I closed my eyes and sighed, "Just don't."

I could see Unc Charles and my mom peeking down the hallway like gophers through the corner of my eye. My mom was showing Unc Charles photos on her phone. They quickly disappeared before Tiana and Debbie turned around. Debbie, Fernando, Avery, and Biscuit took off toward our den with the puppy and other cousins.

I joked with Tiana about her appearance. "Did you get you a set of boobies?" I motioned circles around my chest, "There have been some...developments."

"OMG! You can tell! Are they too big?" Tiana batted her eyes and pointed her heels. "You remember those girls used to make fun of me for being so flat chested? Ugh! Debbie calls me scary mommy," Tiana laughed.

39

"You know mom is gonna say something. She's given her advice to every person in this house but herself."

Saben and Tiana guided me on how to manage the evening as my demeanor became more fidgety. We decided that the goal of the evening was to avoid subjects that lead to Dad. This would be impossible with the five-year anniversary of his death coming up tomorrow.

We decided that I would exit the room for a phone call if my dad was brought up. Then, Saben would text me when the conversation shifted. Within a few minutes, my mom and Unc Charles brisked down the hallway with cordial smiles and glasses full of wine, greeting Tiana.

My relationship with Unc Charles revolved around Thanksgiving and Christmas. I had heard stories of how he and my dad grew up on welfare, which made their college graduation more serious, but I was unaware of the inner-workings of his life. He had never been married, no kids (officially), and had developed a gambling and alcohol problem after the corner of an industrial refrigerator rolled into his eye.

Having discovered that Unc Charles was likely my biological father, any hope for a relationship was not possible or desired. Unc Charles was embarrassing and not the type of person I would seek out in a crowded room. We were related by blood, and that was it.

Despite this, Unc Charles was a talented pianist and singer. He had a raspy screaming blues voice with a soulful burn, reminiscent of Sam Cooke. Unc Charles had sung *At Last* by Etta James at my wedding. By the end of the song, the whole chapel was drowning in tears. He also sang at Dad's funeral. There's a piece of me that could not wait to hear Unc Charles sing every Christmas since Avery and Biscuit had become his biggest fans.

Before dinner, the family gathered around my grand piano, which was swarming with wreaths and shiny ornaments. Unc Charles played the first chords of *The First Noel* followed by a stunning vocal run. For fear that I would hear something in his voice worth forgiving, I left the living room.

TOAST TO ART

"Trey, will you say grace?" my mom sneered as everyone began to settle around the table.

Saben smiled and nodded at me in polite agreement. I called Avery, Biscuit, Fernando, and the other kids to join hands with the adults. Before beginning to pray, I reminded myself not to reference my dad's loss.

"Dear God..." I paused. "I thank you for my wife, my kids, my sister, Debbie, Fernando, and Gammy, and our new puppy. I thank you for my home and this food before us. I ask you to continue to bless us." I opened my eyes and could see my mom's smiling morph into a frown, displeased with the prayer. Unc Charles had begun testing the mashed potatoes while Gammy licked the roof of her mouth in anticipation of her dentures.

I continued, "I ask you to spare the hearts of those who seek to deceive us—liars, cheaters, and false prophets that lurk in the shadows of our lives. The shadow of the truth, Lord. I ask you to purge them. Shine light on their evil ways this Christmas. Expose those who do not have our best interest at heart. Amen."

The living room filled with silence, making awkward Debbie's gulp very audible to everyone. Avery and Biscuit stared at me with blank faces. I heard the puppy peeing somewhere close by.

For the next thirty minutes, the family began to eat. My heart pounded in anticipation of what Unc Charles and my mother would say as they began to drink.

Soon forty minutes had passed. An hour had passed. I sat and ate quieter than usual. Saben placed her hand on my knee, which was beginning to tap.

Biscuit cried out.

"Biscuit, what's wrong, hun?"

"Avery said I couldn't play Playstation with him and Fernando after dinner," Biscuit replied.

"Ave, share with your brother!" my tone sterner than usual.

My mom smiled, placing her hands under her chin. "Biscuit reminds me so much of Art when he was that age, minus the...you know. May he rest in peace."

"Trey, should we do a toast for Art? Tomorrow will be five years since I lost my baby brother." Uncle Charles began to pour champagne into everyone's glass. Everyone agreed to the toast.

"Toast to *Art*?" I asked bitingly.

"Yeah, his anniversary is tomorrow." Unc Charles coughed loudly to clear his throat of mucus and food.

"You haven't said one thing about your father tonight," my mom interjected.

I had finally been activated.

"Some fake muthaf," I said under my breath to Saben.

Saben grabbed my knee under the table before I could finish my sentence. Gammy had heard what I said, glaring at me. Saben motioned for Avery, Biscuit, and Fernando to get the puppy and go upstairs to play Playstation.

"Go now, please. Leave the plates," Saben told the kids.

"Yay!!" Biscuit said joyously.

"Whatchu say, son?" Uncle Charles said, taking a bite of his dinner roll.

"Toast to *Art?* Are you serious right now?" I had had enough of these people.

"Trey, honey...Kim from work called while you were in the kitchen and said to call her ASAP," Saben motioned for me to take her cell.

I stood up from the table. Everyone watched as I walked to the closet underneath our staircase to get a large half-full black garbage bag. I removed items from the bag. A picture of our family, Dad's portrait, and his college journal fell out.

I threw the journal at my mother. Page twelve. She furrowed her eyebrows before putting on her glasses to read. No-one spoke for several seconds as my mom read. I could hear Tiana and Debbie whispering. The guests looked on in confusion.

"Who is dad talking about?"

"What?" my mom asked.

I watched her mind strategize for something smooth to say. "Which girlfriend named *Susan* confessed that she slept with his brother and became pregnant forty-one years ago?"

Debbie gasped loudly.

"Jesus!" Gammy called out. The guests began to chatter with each other.

"What is this?" my mom asked surprisingly like she had forgotten to pay a past due bill and had gotten charged a late fee. Gammy attempted to look at the journal over her arm. My mom pulled it back.

I began to recite what I could remember on page twelve.

"Today, my girlfriend of one year, SUSAN, confessed that she slept with my brother and is pregnant. She is scared of her parents and wants to get married immediately. She said she loved me. I don't know why my brother," I pointed to Unc Charles, "did this to me."

I laughed hysterically, "Is Uncle Charles my father?"

"Oh my God!" my mom shouted out loudly. "Where is this coming from? Why would you do this on your dad's anniversary? He would be so ashamed by how you're acting."

Everyone looked down at their plates—fury built inside me like gas on a fire. My mother sat frozen. I could hear the kids giggling upstairs.

I slammed my fist on the table. The dishware rattled. A champagne glass fell, shattering into pieces, causing Gammy to jump. The kids and the puppy looked on from the top of the stairs.

"You're upsetting Gammy," my mom said.

"Is Uncle Charles my father?!"

My body trembled like the first moments of a rolling earthquake. I started to sweat profusely. Saben reached for my arm; I pulled it back aggressively. Family members began to call their kids downstairs to leave. I could hear Biscuit beginning to cry.

"I'm gonna ask you again. Is Uncle Charles, my father?"

I looked over at Unc Charles, whose chin was resting on his belly.

48

"Well, are you gonna say something or what?" Debbie blurted out.

My mom looked at Debbie with an evil eye, "Do I look like I report to you?"

Debbie stood up, hitting her fist against her palm at my mom. "You been mad doggin' me since I stepped in here." Tiana pulled Debbie back into her seat.

"It's always bitches like you got the most to say, doin' the most," Debbie continued.

"Debra!" Tiana pled.

"If you weren't my wife's moms, I'd knock your fake bitch ass out!" The family watched my mom get cussed out before Debbie stormed out of the dining room.

I looked at Tiana in disbelief, "*Wife*, Tiana? Really?"

Gammy wailed before beginning to pray.

"I was gonna tell you today," Tiana cautioned.

"Wow, you're just like them- fake." I nodded in disbelief.

I panted, losing breath, my eyes pooled with scorching tears. I placed my hands on my head. "Uncle Charles..."

I could barely utter the words, "Are you my father? I need to know. Someone, please tell me."

Time stopped for what felt like hours.

"I am."

I fell into my chair, overwhelmed with emotion.

"Of course he is," Debbie said walking back into the room. "I coulda told you that."

"Wait a second. Art raised him, Charlie. Don't do that to my son," my mom said.

My mom and Unc Charles began to bicker over Gammy's head.

"Charles, you're makin' Gammy upset."

"Girl, don't use me. I'm fine," Gammy responded. "Sho' looks like Art's writing in the journal, too." Gammy rolled her eyes.

Saben rubbed my back. I spoke across the table to my mother, "You have one job. To help your kids survive. You watched me scramble around, burying my dad, knowing he was not my father. And if it weren't for this journal, you never planned to tell me."

"Honey, I understand you are angry, but now is not the time. And it wasn't *all* me." My mom got up from her seat to come to my side of the table.

"When is the time, mom? Forty more years?"

My mom persisted, "I was a young girl. Charles came on to me, and I didn't know what to do. Everything I have done has been to protect this family."

Unc Charles injected, "Came on to you? Girl, you wouldn't leave me alone, then made me give you money for twenty years to pay for their college. So it's *me* who protects this family." He coughed.

"Get out of my house," my voice choked in anger.

"You gave your *brother* money on your own volition. I never wanted your drug, gambling money for my kids. I told Art not to accept anything from you," my mom responded.

"Drug money? Is that what you call it now? Warned Art about you from day one. You always have been and will be trash."

Cousins and family members sat in disbelief, everyone looking at Gammy and my mom.

My mom paused for several seconds before continuing, "I'm not the only woman you raped, Charles."

"Lady, you have lost your god damn mind. Rebuke here!" Unc Charles began to yell repeatedly. "Rebuke here!" He began to recite scripture, "The wicked are estranged from the womb; they go astray from birth, speaking *lies. Lies.*"

Several family members began to pack up.

"Haha, you supposed to be Jesus now?" my mom screamed, laughing.

"Trey, listen to me. I know it's hard for you to understand, but I did the right thing. I was attacked. I was embarrassed. You know my father had a temper, " my mom continued. "Gammy, tell him about daddy."

"I'm too old to be worried about what you doin'," Gammy said.

"Trey, son, me and your daddy was close as ever before your mama got involved. We wanted to tell you, but she blackmailed me and said she would say all this rubbish if I said anything. Jesus knows my heart. Do you remember I joined you and your pops for your 16th birthday?" Unc Charles said. "We were gonna tell you."

"I believe you," Debbie said to Uncle Charles.

"Bitch nobody asked you," my mom responded.

"Call me a bitch again," Debbie shouted. "Say it again, and Imma knock that dollar-tree wig off your big ass head. How your face on your chin?"

"Ooo" one of the cousins responded.

"HIJA DE LAS MIL PUTAS (Daughter of a thousand whores)," Debbie scoffed.

"Get out!" my voice choked. Biscuit tugged at my leg. "NOW! Everyone out! GET OUTTA MY HOUSE!"

Everyone hurried to collect their items and left the house.

"I didn't want you to find out like this," my mom begged.

"OUT!" I hollered.

"It's because you did it," Debbie taunted. The women continued to argue as everyone left the house.

"D-dad," Biscuit said.

"Stop, Caleb! Clean up that dog piss now!" I yelled. Biscuit eyes expanded. He shivered in fear.

MOTHER & SON

Many months went by. I hadn't spoken to my mom or Unc Charles since Christmas. Saben and I had gotten pregnant and were expecting our third child's arrival in six weeks.

My mom had reached out to me numerous times, but all that had occurred felt irreparable. Unc Charles did not contact me once. Conversation felt useless. The more time went by, the deeper I understood that the stories I was told were not only false, but a masquerade-ball of Decepticons, all of whom presented themselves as eternally perfect.

Unaware that Saben was pregnant again, Tiana posted photos of the baby shower on her social media for my mom to see. Gammy called me to tell me that my mom felt exiled and had fallen into a low-grade depression.

Gammy called me one evening. "Trey, listen to your Gammy. You only get one mom, and I know how she is, ok? Can you find it in your heart to listen to what she has to say?"

"I'm not ready yet," I replied. "Forty-two years, Gammy. And she knew dad was sick. I've been robbed. I need more time."

"Have you spoken to your Unc Charles?"

"About what, Gammy?" I continued. "Just because he's technically my father doesn't mean I want a relationship with him. He should call me."

She continued, "There will be people in your life you have to forgive many, many times, and sometimes it's yo mama. Trust me, I forgive your grandpa, his whole got-damn life."

Gammy continued, "I hope you can find it in your heart to hear what they have to say, Trey. And maybe forgive them. For your own happiness and closure."

On the 10th of November, Saben and I brought our third child, our first girl, Amaya Janese Amana, home. Amaya

Janese was fierce, contemplative, and not a fan of visitors and prying eyes over her small body. Tiana, her wife Debbie, and Fernando had come over to meet Amaya on Thanksgiving Day. Tiana called me into my office to speak privately.

"Mom asked me to give this to you." Tiana handed me a white envelope with my name written on it in cursive. Nearly a year had passed since I had seen and spoken to my mom or Unc Charles.

"I had a conversation with her. You should read it. She understands if you never want to speak to her again," Tiana said. "It sounds like she's trying."

I scoffed under my breath.

After going back and forth with Saben for three nights, I finally poured a cup of Chamomile tea and took the letter into my office to read it.

Dear son:

I was so wrong. I've thought many nights about how to begin to explain to you why I chose to hide the truth for forty years. I didn't know how to have this conversation.

Back then was not like it is now—This new generation lives without consequence. I rather risk the secret being found out than bringing attention to me and shame to my parents. This was a normal expectation of children in my day, and I genuinely feel like I made the right decision at the time.

Pride would not allow me to step foot into a therapist's office for almost seventy years, so I want you to know that I have seen a counselor every week since February. I should have seen someone when the pregnancy occurred. But getting help was so taboo fifty years ago. People would think you're crazy if you say you need help.

But, I see how my upbringing and choices have affected me as a mother and grandmother. While this hurts, I must admit that I am relieved that I have the opportunity to discuss this.

I was afraid of my dad, afraid of myself, and desired male attention that felt different. Art and Charlie made me feel seen. They were handsome, and their family was kind, hardworking, and perfect compared to mine. I never considered the long term effects. It seemed like the right thing for us to keep it quiet. Now, I see how I took away the chance for you to know your dad and Charlie on a deeper level.

I wanted to tell you about this when Art passed away but could not muster the courage. I know that's difficult to understand, but I've carried this a long time, too. I thought I would be dead by the time this came to light.

Carrying this weight felt normal. I see how I've redirected my pain onto others for years. I understand how I have worn a façade to protect the little girl inside.

I can't bring Art back, but don't ever doubt that he loved you. You were his son. Charlie loves you deeply, too. And I hope you find it in your heart to speak to him and forge a relationship.

I have never told you how proud I am of you. I am so proud! You're hardworking, you take care of your family, and you're resilient in every way. Trey, you are the prototype of a man and a son. Avery and Caleb are in love with you. Saben is in love with you. You carry the torch for the Amanas in a remarkable way. I am so proud of you, Trey. So proud to be your mom.

I don't blame you for not speaking to me, and I don't blame you for holding your family away from me.

I hope to hear from you sooner than later and to meet the baby.

Love, Mom

"Sabe!" I called for Saben throughout the house. "Just read it!"

"Ok, I can tell she's been gettin' help; she actually apologized! But that's her side..."

I called for Saben loudly throughout the house. "But what does Unc Charles' have to say? What did he mean when he said he gave her money for twenty years? What is dad's side? They can plot and say anything they want."

I found Saben sitting in the kitchen, clutching her cell-phone.

"Sabe."

Saben looked up at me. She bit her bottom lip, nodding her head as tears flowed from her closed eyes. She held her phone close to her chest.

"What is it, babe?" I kissed Saben's soft cheeks. She motioned for me to sit down, wiping away the shiny tears.

"Hun?" I asked.

"Your mom."

"What happened?"

"Uncle Charles. They found him in his bathroom...Uncle Charles is dead."

HOW MANY CHANCES

I wish I could say that I read the letter, woke up the next day, and forgave my mom, dad, and Uncle Charles for everything they had done and the secrets they had kept. I wish I could tell you that my mom transformed into the grandma of the year overnight. But I can't.

Unc Charles's sudden death, which was not sudden-he had been diagnosed with heart disease, didn't tell anyone, and died of congestive heart failure-emphasized the importance of me making a drastic decision about how this family moved forward.

At Unc Charles's funeral, I spoke to my mom. I told her that I had received her letter and accepted her apology. She met Amaya briefly, who she adored. With her apology, I was unsure if my mom could be trusted. My dad and Unc Charles were dead, and I only had her words to go by.

I wanted my kids to grow up believing that truth and character matter. While Susan Amana *is* their grandmother, she is not a stand out example of truth and character. My kids are not of an age to decipher the real from the fake. I decided to restrict interactions with my mom to holidays only until they could hear from their grandma's lips, in her own words, what happened and make an independent decision to engage with her.

As everyone left the gravesite, I invited Avery, almost twelve years old, and Biscuit, practically nine years old, to stand with me by my dad and Unc Charles' graves. Saben returned to the limo to nurse Amaya. My mother and other family drove away.

"Guys, these are two men who made very different choices and lived very different lives." Nervously, Avery and Biscuit stared at the graves as I explained the choices my dad and Unc

Charles made. "Both of them hurt a lot of people. They both hurt Grandma; they both hurt me..."

Avery suggested that he would not be alive had anything gone different, and we would not have our family. Biscuit identified that I had not gotten the opportunity to talk to grandpa or Uncle Charles about anything, which was not fair.

Biscuit asked, "Are you still mad at Grandma?"

"Grandma is on a long time out." I continued, "I want you both to know that we don't get to choose a lot of what happens to us in life. We don't choose our parents. We don't choose who we are, but we choose who we become and how we react."

Two bright beams of sunlight pierced through the trees' leaves onto my dad and Charles's tombstones. Brilliant white clouds that had overtaken the sky shifted to the water-colored pastel pinks, blues, and emerald I had noticed in Fisherman's Lake.

"Be humble and kind because you never know the full story of why people act the way they do. Do you understand?"

I looked down at Avery, his eyes sincere, wondering what this all meant to his middle school world. Biscuit beginning to choke up, wrapped his arm around my leg, "I still love you, Dad, no matter who your father is."

Sunlight accentuated the colors of the large bouquets of mums, snapdragons, and daises that Avery and Biscuit placed on the tombstones.

Some days I wake up, and there's a moment, at least sixty seconds after I open my eyes, that I feel the pain of the past has melted away. Like I'm ready to fully forgive and move on. But then, as consciousness settles in, the relief vanishes.

I still have more questions than answers, and every day that passes by, the uncertainty compiles, and the truth feels harder to reach. I can't seem to shake the guilt I have about Uncle Charles. How reckless was I to let the opportunity slip away? To let my anger and my disgust outweigh the need for clarity I craved for. Clarity is a treasure.

Maybe my mom has changed. Perhaps she hasn't. Many nights I wonder if her letter and therapy sessions are enough for me to bear the heavy load of being graceful to her. One letter and a year of therapy later - she can be trusted? Forty years. Forty-two years of silence.

Had I not discovered my dad's journal, she would have never said anything. That's just who she is. And if she died tomorrow, I would regret not moving forward and being the bigger person. But what if I'm tired of being the bigger person? I want to believe that I could have handled knowing the truth, but maybe I could not have—they say ignorance is bliss for a reason.

It's true, Arthur, Susan, and Charles were from a different generation with different social challenges and pressures. Single moms or "babies out of wedlock," little boys painting their nails, fake breasts, etc., *did* draw attention in a time when the need to conform and be integrated into white supremacy directly affected one's livelihood. Why make your life harder by admitting a mistake or being openly complex when you're already black in America? I get it.

But where is the line? How much of one's toxic behavior will we allow them to hide behind "a generation?" How much toxicity will we allow to hide behind "their life's oppression?" Where is the accountability for actions and words in this now moment?

I once heard a quote that said the secret to a good morning is to watch the sunrise with an open heart. Beyond the deception and dysfunction, perhaps my lesson is to learn to approach each day with an open heart, simply because the sun, the *day* itself, is a gift. Another chance for unfoldment. Another opportunity to write a new chapter—to change the ending to the story and insert the twist.

I will do better today and show my kids what forgiveness looks like by not letting my mother or the memory of my dad or Uncle Charles determine how my sun rises.

I can not erase what has happened, and it will be hard to be kind when I've been deceived. Still, I must show my sons what accountability and responsibility look like in hopes that they will choose better if such dishonor lands on their doorstep.

If you know better, you do better.

THE END

Ross Victory is a singer/songwriter turned author from Southern California. He is the author of the award-winning non-fiction books *Views from the Cockpit: The Journey of a Son* and *Panorama: The Missing Chapter.* When Ross isn't writing or singing, he enjoys traveling and cars.

Learn more: rossvictory.com

Books available by Ross Victory

also available in
ebook